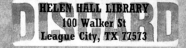
To all of the storks who have
to leave their nests, hoping
to find a welcoming home
where their dreams can
come true.

CUENTO
DE LUZ

To the people who accompanied me on this journey.
- María Quintana Silva -

For Philippe and the three cats.
- Marie-Noëlle Hébert -

Waterproof and tear resistant
Produced without water, without trees and without bleach
Saves 50% of energy compared to normal paper

Kalak's Journey
Text © 2018 María Quintana Silva
Illustrations © 2018 Marie-Noëlle Hébert
This edition © 2018 Cuento de Luz SL
Calle Claveles, 10 | Urb. Monteclaro | Pozuelo de Alarcón | 28223 | Madrid | Spain
www.cuentodeluz.com
Title in Spanish: El viaje de Kalak
English translation by Jon Brokenbrow
Printed in PRC by Shanghai Chenxi Printing Co., Ltd. December 2017, print number 1625-1
ISBN: 978-84-16733-44-6

KALAK'S JOURNEY

María Quintana Silva

Marie-Noëlle Hébert

Kalak lived with his parents, his brothers and sisters, and a hundred other storks, in a part of the world where the nests were old, the roofs were damaged, the earth was dry, and there was never enough food for everyone. One day, they all decided to leave, and fly off to another part of the world.

"We'll be able to eat lots of yummy worms!" said his oldest brother.

"But what about our nest?" asked Kalak, as he skimmed over a cloud.

"We'll build a better one!" said another one of his brothers.

"We'll be so happy!" said his sister, as she soared past him.

They flew for hours, for days, for weeks…
It was a long, long journey, and there was little time for rest. Kalak's tummy started to rumble. He hadn't eaten anything for ages.

"Are we there yet?" he asked.
"Be patient," said his father. "We still have to cross the sea."
"Keep going, Kalak!" said his mother. "Stay close!"

Suddenly, the storks began to fly lower and lower. Beneath the clouds, a vast expanse of blue appeared, which would be difficult to cross.

Kalak flapped his wings, as he began to feel more and more exhausted. But he could not rise back up into the air without the warm currents that helped him to fly over the land. The little bird gradually started to fall behind the rest of the flock.

Kalak flew lower and lower, until his wings almost touched the water. Far from the rest of the flock, he struggled to stay above the waves. He could drown if just one of his feathers got wet.

"Will we really find another home?" thought Kalak, as he gazed towards the point where the sea and the sky met on the horizon.

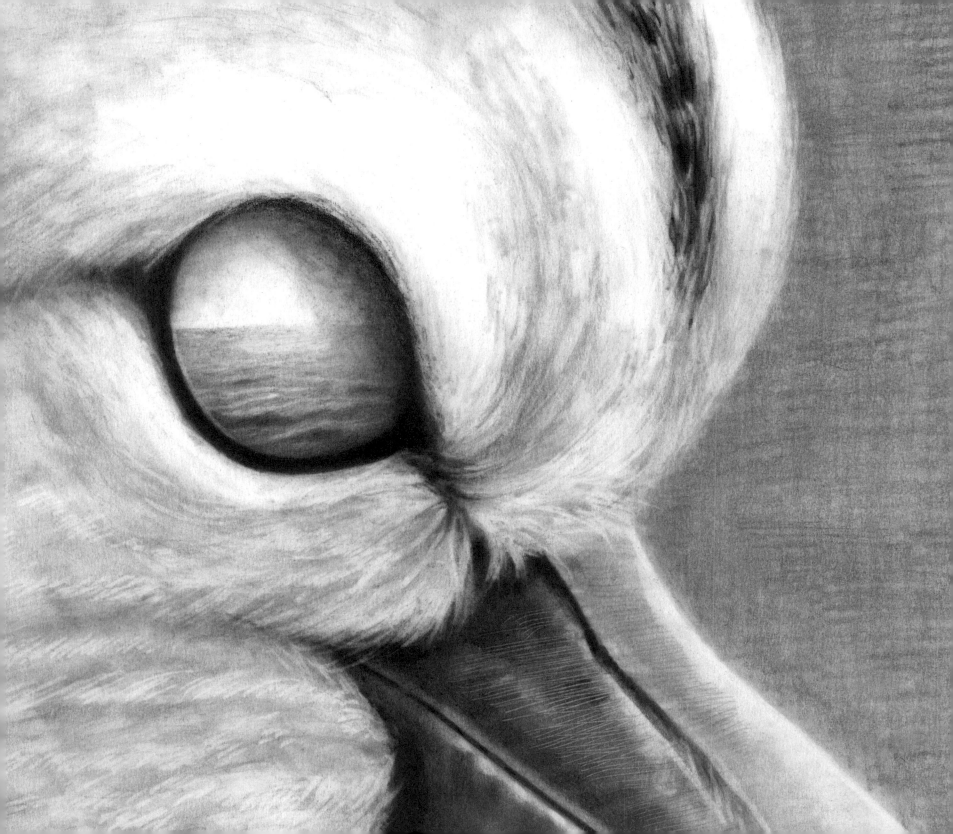

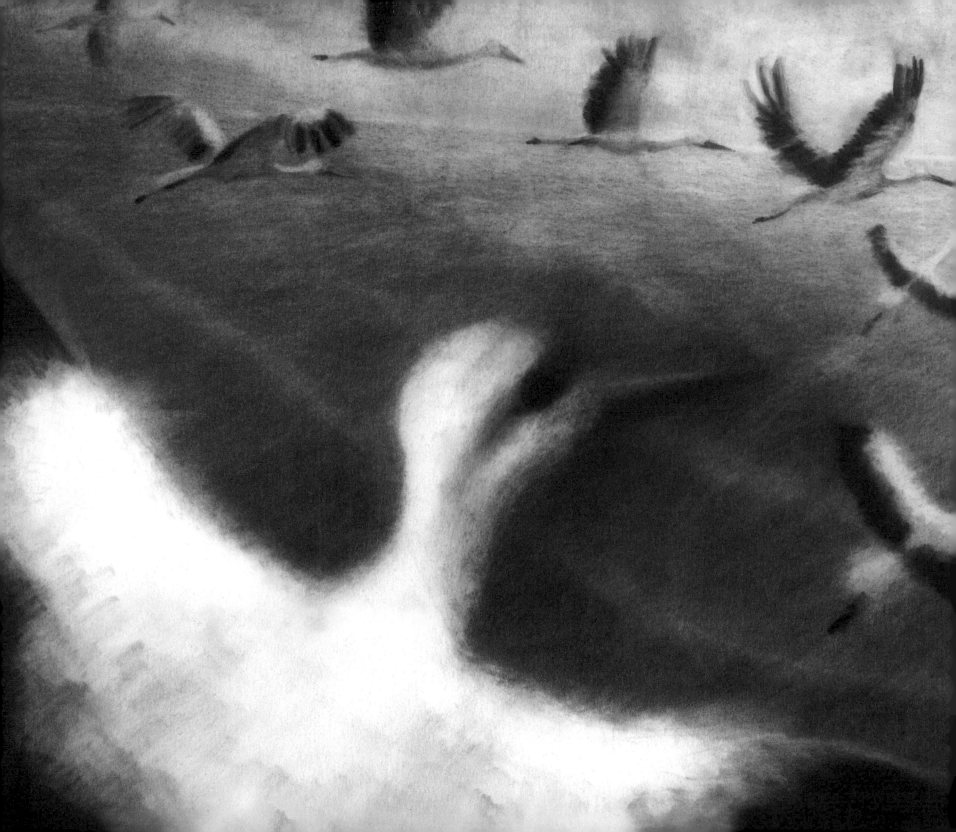

Finally, the land came into sight. When
Kalak reached it at last, warm air currents
helped Kalak to rise above the rooftops,
until he caught up with the flock once again.

"Mom! Dad!" he called, but there was no reply. There was no sign of his parents, or his brothers and sisters.

"How am I going to find our new nest?" he asked himself, as he flew around in circles.

The sky was slowly filling with huge, gray clouds, and the storks suddenly found themselves in the middle of a great storm.

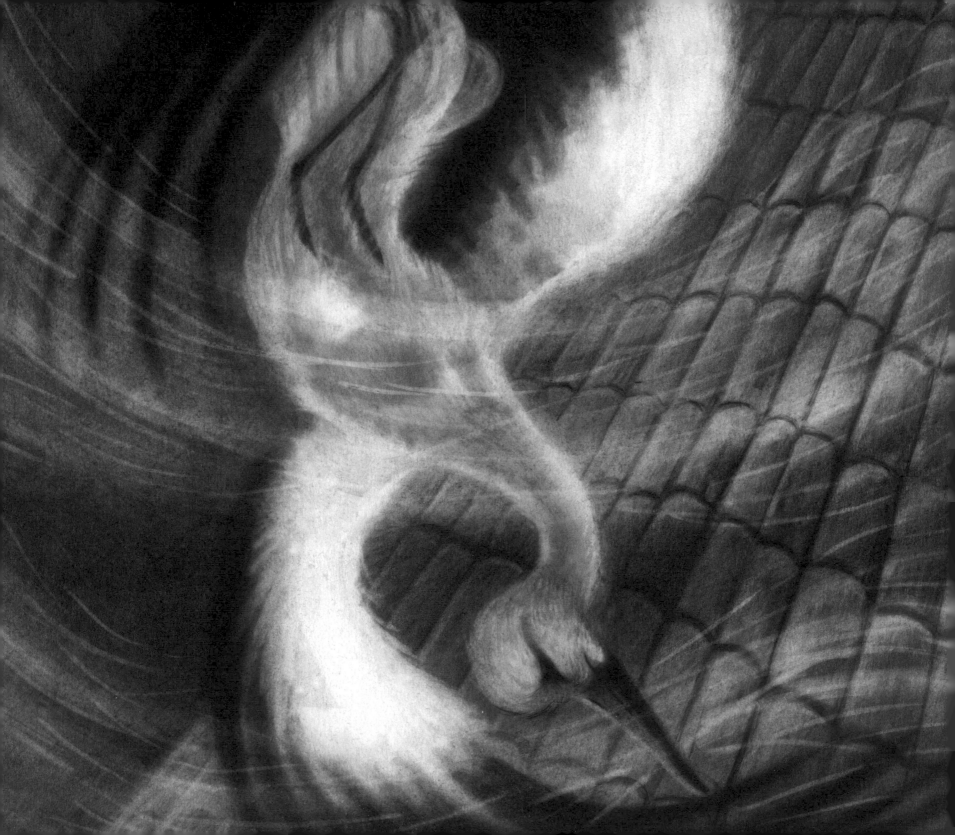

The wind blew Kalak around like a leaf, far away from the rest of the flock. He fought to stay in the air, until a huge gust threw him against the roof of a house.

Lost, alone, and injured, Kalak wrapped himself in his wet feathers as thunder and lighting boomed all around him. He thought about his old nest, and fell fast asleep.

He woke to the smell of fresh grass. All around him, elegant storks had built beautiful nests on the other roofs.

"Get off our roof!" croaked two of
the local storks.

"Sorry, I'm just looking for my
family," said Kalak, nervously. "Do
you know where my nest is?"

"There's no room for you here,"
said one of the storks.

"You're not welcome here," said his companion, and they both pushed Kalak towards the edge of the roof.

Kalak felt the pain from his injured wing as he tried to stay put, but the effort was too much, and he fell off the roof.

"That's not very nice of you!"
yelled Kalak, as he fluttered to the ground.

Kalak lay in the wet grass all alone, without knowing what to do, or where to go.

Suddenly, another stork landed next to him, and wrapped her wings around Kalak in a warm embrace. Then she flew off again, and Kalak followed her, hopping and flying as best he could.

"Kal-ak! Kal-ak! Kal-ak!"
Someone was calling his name from three streets away.

"Kal-ak! Kal-ak! Kal-ak!"

called his family, happily raising their beaks into the air, hugging him and thanking the kind stork.

So now Kalak, his family, and all of his flock live in a new home, where there are plenty of worms for everyone. Many local storks helped them to build new nests, and Kalak's tummy has stopped rumbling.

Kalak is a stork of the world, free to fly high and discover new horizons.